Dear Parent:
Your child's love of reading starts here!

I Can Read Books have introduced children to the joy of reading since 1957. Featuring award-winning authors and illustrators and a fabulous cast of beloved characters, I Can Read Books set the standard for beginning readers. From books your child reads with you to the first books they read alone, there are I Can Read Books for every stage of reading:

SHARED READING
Basic language, word repetition, and whimsical illustrations, ideal for sharing with your emergent reader

BEGINNING READING
Short sentences, familiar words, and simple concepts for children eager to read on their own

READING WITH HELP
Engaging stories, longer sentences, and language play for developing readers

READING ALONE
Complex plots, challenging vocabulary, and high-interest topics for the independent reader

ADVANCED READING
Short paragraphs, chapters, and exciting themes for the perfect bridge to chapter books

Every child learns in a different way and at their own speed. Some read through each level in order. Others go back and forth between levels and read favorite books again and again. You can help your young reader improve and become more confident by encouraging their own interests and abilities.

A lifetime of discovery begins with the magical words, **"I Can Read!"**

For my dear friend Janet
—S.W.

For Hilary, Emily, and Mallory—
three sweet girls who never sneeze!
—J.M.

HarperCollins®, 🐑®, and I Can Read Book® are trademarks of HarperCollins Publishers Inc.

Library of Congress Cataloging-in-Publication Data
Weeks, Sarah.
  Baa-choo! / by Sarah Weeks ; illustrated by Jane Manning.— 1st ed.
    p. cm. — (An I Can Read book)
  Summary: When Sam the lamb has trouble sneezing, the other animals try to help.
  ISBN 0-06-029236-9 — ISBN 0-06-029237-7 (lib. bdg.) — ISBN 0-06-443740-X (pbk.)
  [1. Sneezing—Fiction. 2. Sheep—Fiction. 3. Domestic animals—Fiction. 4. Stories in rhyme.] I. Manning, Jane K., ill. II. Title. III. Series.
PZ8.3.W4125Bae 2004
[E]—dc22   2003017549

❖

An I Can Read Book™

by Sarah Weeks
pictures by Jane Manning

HarperCollins*Publishers*

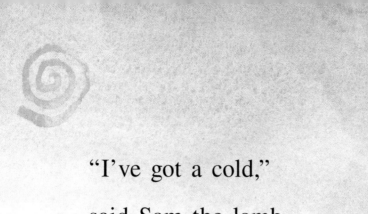

"I've got a cold,"

said Sam the lamb.

"I'm going to sneeze,

indeed I am."

His little nose twitched,

and wiggled,

and itched.

"Baa . . . ahh . . ."

No *choo*.

"I've got the *ahhh*
but not the *choo*.
No, no, this sneeze
will never do."

9

"Can someone help me,

help me please,

to find the ending

of my sneeze?"

"I'll tickle your nose
with a feather, and then
I'm sure you'll sneeze,"
said Gwen the hen.

11

She tickled his nose.

Sam said,

"Here goes!

Baa . . . ahhh . . ."

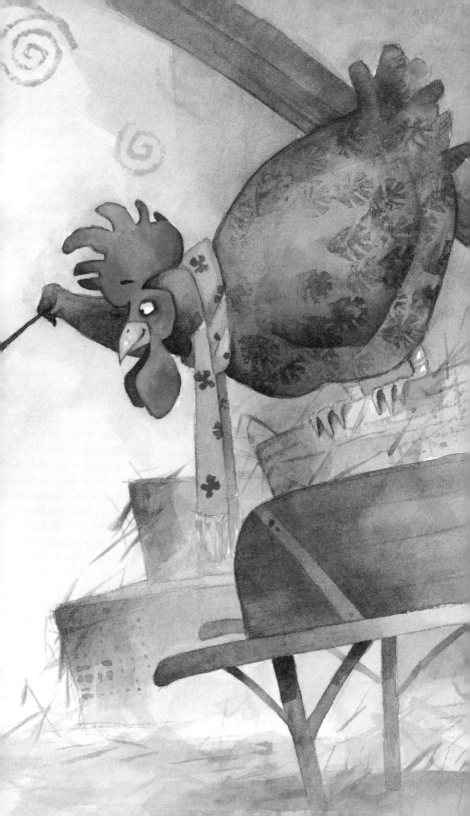

No *choo.*

"Gee," said Sam.

"That didn't feel right.

It felt . . . almost,

but then . . . not quite.

"Can someone help me,

help me please,

to find the ending

of my sneeze?"

Sig the pig said,

"I have a plan.

We'll sprinkle some pepper

in front of this fan.

"Sam, stand over there,

and stick out your nose,

and sniff wherever

the pepper blows."

17

So Sam sniffed,

and snorted,

and snuffed.

Huffed and puffed

with his nose all stuffed.

18

The pepper went flying.

Sam kept trying.

"Baa . . . ahhh . . ."

No *choo*.

"Gee," said Sam.

"This isn't much fun.

Why can't this sneeze

be over and done?

"Can someone help me,

help me please,

to find the ending

of my sneeze?"

Franny Nannygoat

came by

and said that she

would like to try.

"I'll kick up dust!"

And so she did,

with a bit of help

from her little kid.

The dust was thick.

Sam started to wheeze,

and then at last

he started to sneeze.

This time it was bigger.

And louder and longer.

Instead of stopping,

it just got stronger.

"Quick! Everyone do

whatever you can!"

Gwen grabbed her feather.

Sig turned on his fan.

Together they tickled

and sprinkled and kicked

to make the big sneeze grow.

Then someone cried,

"Look out! Look out!

I think he's going to blow!"

27

Then Sam the lamb

let out a sneeze

that raised the roof

and shook the trees.

Believe me when
I say it's true,
no lamb has sneezed
a louder *choo*.

29

"Thank you, friends,"

said Sam the lamb,

"for coming to the rescue."

Sam heard them say,

from far away,

"You're welcome, Sam, and—"

"Bless you!"